Jordan's Quest

Small Purpose Big Destiny

DAVY LIU

KENDUFILMS

Written and illustrated
by Davy Liu

Grateful acknowledgement to Nancy Sanders for her
creative input and insight.

Special thanks to my mother and father, my wife, Joan,
my constant support; Dr. Mark Arvidson: Compass Bible
Church families, St. Norbert School, Hui-Fen Wang, Sheila
Tseng, Stephen Parolini, the support and the prayers of my
friends.

D.L.

©2009 by Kendu LLC. All rights reserved.
Published in the United States by Kendu Films, Inc.
27068 La Paz RD #543, Aliso Viejo, CA 92656
www.kendufilms.com

ISBN 978-0-9825050-3-8
Printed in Korea

For the King of kings

"*P*ick me! Pick me!" Jordan brayed

as the guests walked into the stable yard.

Jordan pranced and danced, and did his

best to catch their eye. But the guests

stopped next to the horses instead.

Jordan hung his head. Every day it was

the same. Guests always chose horses

or camels as their ride for the city tour.

Nobody ever picked Jordan.

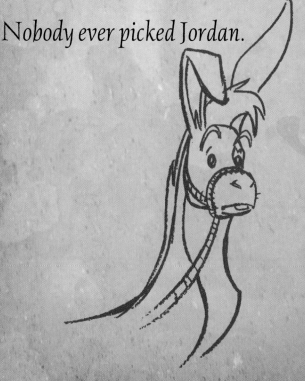

Jordan's Guest

"Hey, Jordan!" squealed the piglet twins, Jen and Tyle, as they ran up to Jordan.

"Watcha' doin' today?" asked Jen.
"Wanna' play?" asked Tyle.
Benny the lamb trotted over. "Let's play pretend!"

Jen and Tyle climbed onto Jordan's back.
"Look at us!" squealed Jen and Tyle, bouncing up and down.

"Look at me!" brayed Jordan. "I'm carrying guests on the city tour!"

"Stop all this hullabaloo, Jordan," the goat complained. "If I were a guest, I wouldn't pick someone with short legs and long ears."

"That's a job for horses and camels," said the cow, "and my job is to provide milk."

"Mine too," said the goat.

"Your mother carries sticks," the cow continued. "The sheep give wool. All the animals work hard to serve our master."

"Even my little Benny has a purpose," said the sheep. "He's been chosen as The One."

"We all have important jobs," the goat sneered. "Except you."

Jordan's Guest

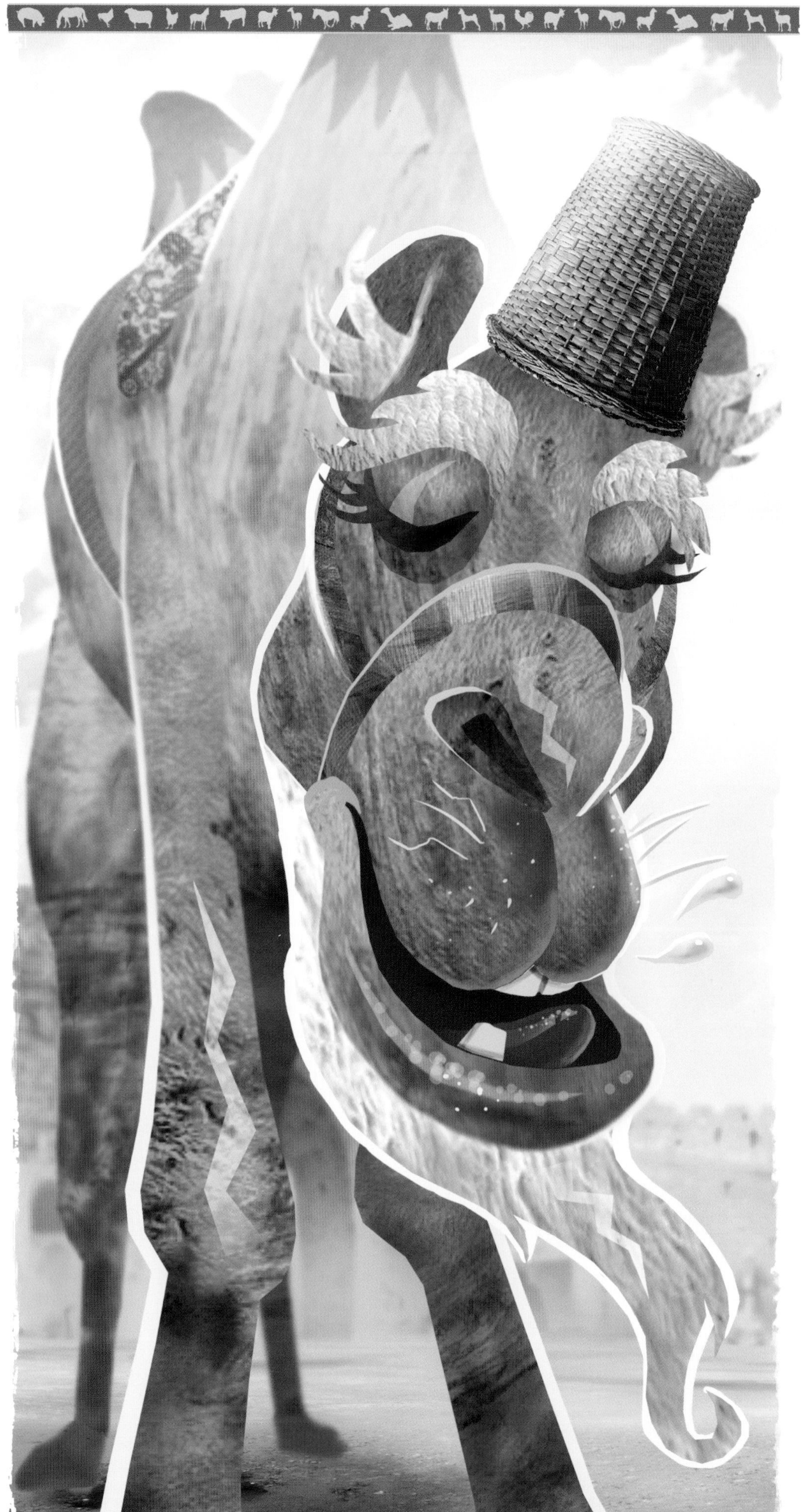

*J*ordan sat down. Jen and Tyle slid off his back.

"Don't be sad," they said. "We still like you."

Just then, Melchior the wise old camel returned to the stable yard.

"Melchior!" Jordan cried. "Why don't I have an important job? What is my purpose? Am I going to be sold?"

Melchior looked down at Jordan with a gentle smile. "Patience, young one," he said. "Each one of us has an important purpose in life. Even if it is small."

*M*elchior settled on the ground.
"You remind me of your father. Small
purpose. Big destiny."

"I do?" Jordan asked. "How do you know
my father? What do you know about
him? Do you know where he is? Tell me!
Tell me!"

"Patience!" Melchior said with a laugh. "I
knew your father when he was just your
size. He wondered about his purpose, too.
But his destiny was to carry a special baby
who was born under a star. After that,
your father and I lived here for years. This
is where he met your mother."

"Will I see him again?" Jordan asked.

"Patience, little one. Patience," said
Melchior.

Jordan was glad to learn more about his
father. But he was also a little sad. He
missed him.

*T*he next morning, Jen and Tyle ran up to Jordan.

"Let's play! Let's play!" they shouted.

"I don't feel like playing today," Jordan said. "I heard something terrible last night."

"What did you hear?" asked Jen.

Jordan blinked back his tears. "The goat said that every year they take away The One to the Palace of Smoke..."

"Benny is The One this year!" Tyle interrupted.

"...and," Jordan continued, "she said that once The One goes to the Palace of smoke, he never comes back."

Jen and Tyle stopped smiling. "When the goat said this," continued Jordan, "even the cow started to cry."

*T*he next morning, the animals came to the well, like they always did.

"Jordan's gone!" Benny shouted.

"Oh stop all that hullabaloo!" grumbled the goat. "Jordan's not..." Suddenly she stopped. "Why, he is gone!"

"Do you think they took him to the Palace of Smoke?" asked the cow.

"But he's not The One," said the sheep.

"My Benny is The One."

Benny looked up at his mother and smiled. But inside he was a little afraid.

"He was probably sold," the goat said, "just like his father."

Sheba the dog ran barking into the stable yard. "Did you hear the news?" Sheba yelped.

"Tell us," the goat insisted.

"An important guest is coming to the city!"

"Who is he?" asked the cow.

"I think he is a king," Sheba said.

Just then, they noticed a small commotion.

Soon a great noise filled the air. It was a happy sound.

"It's a parade!" shouted Jen.

"Let me see, let me see!" said Tyle. Everyone turned toward the sound, trying to get a better view through all those legs.

"Look!" Tyle squealed. "It's Jordan!"

Sheba ran up. "It's him!" he barked.

"Jordan is giving a ride to the most important guest!"

"Hip, hip, hooray for Jordan!" Jen and Tyle shouted.

Melchior stared. "This guest . . . he looks so familiar."

Then, as Jordan and his guest drew near, Melchior recognized the guest and suddenly bowed down.

When Jordan returned to the stable, he was the center of attention! The horses and camels cheered. Jen and Tyle climbed up on Jordan for a piggyback ride just like in the parade.

"What's this?" squealed Jen.

"Look everyone!" Tyle shouted. "Look what happened to Jordan!"

"What is it?" Jordan brayed anxiously.

T here's something on your back," said Jen.

"*I never noticed it before,*" added Tyle.

Jen and Tyle slid off Jordan's back. Melchior moved in closer.

"Hmm…It looks like two sticks," he said. "Two crisscrossed sticks."

"*It's a miracle!*" said one of the horses.

"S top all this hullabaloo," said the goat. "If Jordan's guest was really important he would have ridden on a horse."

"That's right," said one of the horses. "Jordan's guest looked ordinary to me— just like everyone else in the parade."

"And anyway, I don't believe in miracles," the goat continued. "The marks don't mean anything."

Just then the sheep ran up. "Benny is gone! My son is gone!"

"But it's not time yet, is it?" asked the cow.

"No. It isn't time to go to the Palace of Smoke. That's why I'm worried!" The sheep was in tears.

Jordan's heart beat fast in fear.

A few days later, Benny was still missing. Jordan was worried about his good friend. And he was still upset because of what the goat had said about his guest.

Suddenly Sheba ran into the stable yard.

"Did you hear the news?" he barked.

"What news?" all the animals asked.

"They tied up Jordan's guest and took him away!" Sheba said.

"Oh dear, I wonder if they took him away to the Palace of Smoke?" cried the cow.

"*T*his is awful," said Jordan. "Everything is going wrong."

"What should we do?" asked Jen.

"I've got to find Benny," said Jordan.

"We'll come with you," said Tyle.

Within minutes, the three were on their way.

"Benny!" Jordan brayed.

"Benny!" called Jen and Tyle.

By the time the sun was shining high in the sky, they were tired, hungry, and very, very discouraged.

Suddenly, thunder rumbled in the distance and the sky grew dark.

"Wh—what's happening?" cried Jordan.

"It's a storm!" squealed Jen.

"It's as dark as night," squealed Tyle.

"But it's the middle of the day," said Jordan, puzzled.

They all ducked into a nearby cave.

I 'm scared," Jordan said.

"Me, too," said Jen.

"Me, three," said Tyle.

"Me, four!" *a voice echoed behind them.*

"A-A-A-A-AH-AH-AH!"

screamed the three friends.

*J*ordan spun around. "Benny!" he cried. "We found you! We thought something terrible had happened to you."

Benny drew in a shaky breath. "I'm okay," he whispered. "I was trying to find you, Jordan. I thought you were sold. Then I got lost. Now that we're all together again, I feel much better."

"You'll never guess what happened while you were gone. I was in a parade and, look! I got a special mark on my back!"

Jordan showed Benny the crisscrossed marks, and then the four friends talked and talked and talked about all that had happened.

Finally, Jordan said, "Let's go home."

Jordan's Guest

The friends started back, but as nighttime approached, they began to realize they were lost. Jordan couldn't help worrying. How would they find their way home? What would happen when they got there? Would he be sold? Would they take Benny away to the Palace of Smoke, never to return?

As they walked past a hill, they saw an old donkey.

"Jen! Tyle! What are you doing here?" the old donkey asked.

Jordan stopped in his tracks. "You know Jen and Tyle?"

"I just moved into the barn next to them," said the old donkey.

"Whatcha doin' here, Alexander?" asked Tyle.

"It's my job to take down these big sticks," Alexander explained. He turned to look up at the top of the hill.

Jordan followed his gaze. Somehow, just looking at those sticks made him feel sad. And yet...

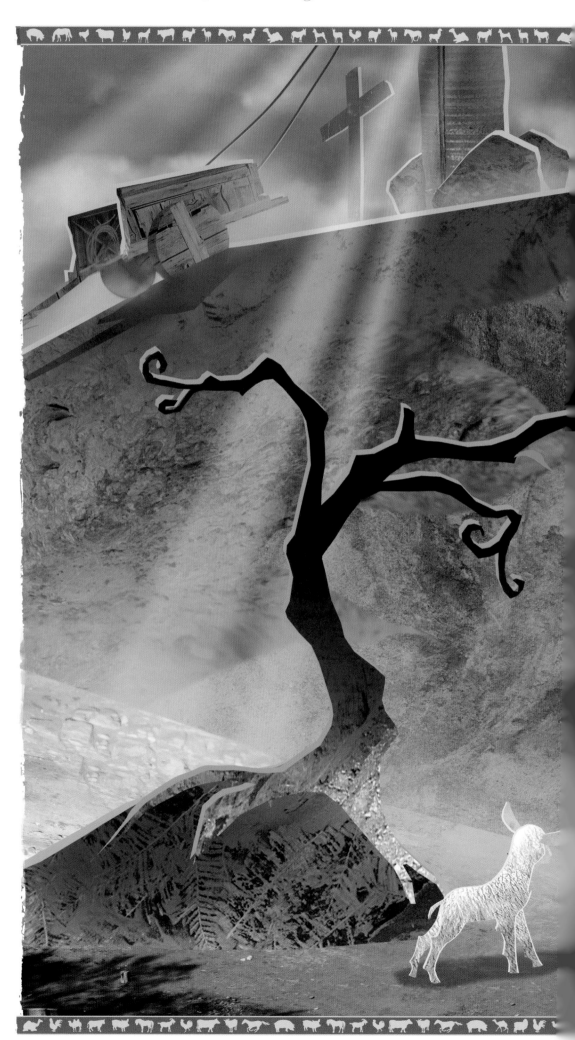

"*T*hose sticks look familiar," said Jen.

"They look like the marks on Jordan's back," added Tyle.

Alexander got very excited. "Jen! Tyle! Pull this blanket off my back," he said. "Do you see? Do you see? I have the same marks! It happened after I saw the birth of a king. I carried his mother to the stable where he was born!"

"A king isn't born in a stable," Benny protested.

"That's what I thought," said Alexander, "until a camel brought him gifts of gold."

"Did that camel follow a star?" Jordan asked.

Alexander nodded.

"I know that camel! It was Melchior!" shouted Jordan. Suddenly tears filled his eyes. "Father! You are my father!" he cried.

*J*ordan's heart felt like it would burst with joy. He had found his father!

A few moments later, Benny spoke up. "This is such good news! But...we're still lost."

"Don't worry. I know the way home," Alexander said, blinking back his tears. "I'll show you."

Jordan hesitated. Then he whispered in his father's ear. "Benny has been chosen as The One."

*Y*ou have nothing to fear," Alexander said. "The important guest took Benny's place. They brought him here to this hill. They put him up on these crisscrossed sticks. Now he is no more."

"I don't understand," said Jordan. "Why did they punish him?"

"Have patience, young one," said Alexander softly.

Jordan stared in surprise. "That's what Melchior said."

Alexander laughed. "So that wise, old camel still gives the same advice?" He smiled. "Those were the exact words Melchior said to me, son. 'Small purpose. Big destiny.'" Alexander looked around. "But now I have work to do. And it's time for you to go home."

The next few days went by in a blur. When he thought about everything that had happened, Jordan felt both happy and sad. He was happy he'd found his father, but he still didn't have anything important to do. He had no purpose. He was afraid he'd be sold.

Sheba the dog ran in, barking, "Good news! Good news! Have you heard the good news?!"

All the animals gathered in wonder.

"What is it, Sheba?" demanded the goat.

"Jordan's guest came back! Someone saw him! It's truly a miracle!"

"Nonsense!" said the goat scornfully.

"It's impossible! No one ever comes back," agreed the cow.

As the animals argued back and forth, a familiar figure walked toward them.

ho could have known a small parade and a guest would bring so much attention? Jordan's fame soon brought many more guests from far, far away. Everyone stood in line hoping to see the miracle of this legendary little donkey and maybe, just maybe touch the crisscrossed marks on his back.

Each word of admiration and clap of applause was a reminder of what Melchior had said. Small purpose. Big destiny. Melchior was right after all!

And Jordan would never be the same again.

Inspired by the historical events
from the books of the Gospels
Matthew, Mark, Luke and John

"The Life of Christ"

"I am the way and the truth and the life"

Jesus

*"For God so loved the world that he gave his one and
only Son, that whoever believes in him shall not perish
but have eternal life."*

John 3:16